Follow the Star

Susan Trede

Illustrated by Claire Jones

Believe!
Susan Trede
2015

LifeRich Publishing is a registered trademark of The Reader's Digest Association, Inc.

LifeRich Publishing books may be ordered through booksellers or by contacting:

LifeRich Publishing
1663 Liberty Drive
Bloomington, IN 47403
www.liferichpublishing.com
1 (888) 238-8637

Because of the dynamic nature of the Internet, any web addresses or links contained in this book may have changed since publication and may no longer be valid. The views expressed in this work are solely those of the author and do not necessarily reflect the views of the publisher, and the publisher hereby disclaims any responsibility for them.

Any people depicted in stock imagery provided by Thinkstock are models, and such images are being used for illustrative purposes only. Certain stock imagery © Thinkstock.

ISBN: 978-1-4897-0534-1(sc)
ISBN: 978-1-4897-0533-4 (e)

Print information available on the last page.

LifeRich Publishing rev. date: 09/04/2015

Dedicated to all my Grandchildren
Love you all!

Thank You to Staci Robinson, Kathleen Kruse and Karen Hansen,
My Wonderful Husband, Tom,
And all our wonderful children who had faith and gave me the encouragement to do this!

And a Special Thank You to Claire and all your wonderful
illustrations! You made my story come to life!

She finished washing the last of the dishes. She would put them away later. Emma had made cookies, pies, loaves of bread and dinner was in the oven now. She took off her apron and sat down in front of the window and saw the picturesque scene. There had been a blizzard the day and night before and the countryside was blanketed with a 10 inch layer of snow. The evergreen trees were flocked with snow and cardinals were sitting on the branches, decorating them with their red color. It was almost dark and soon everyone would be coming in to eat. She had a crocheted scarf she had just finished to give to her husband, Nicholas, later. It was a tradition they had started when they had been married a year and continued every year on their anniversary, December, 24.

Nicholas was in the workshop, finishing up some carved toys. He had carved a mother and father with a baby and he did not know why. He took special pride in the detail. The baby was not in a regular baby bed or crib. The baby was definitely a boy and he was lying in a straw filled bed. The mother and father were kneeling by the bed. He hoped Emma would like them. They had never had any children but were happy and content with their lives. All of their helpers got a special meal tonight and Emma had been working on it all day. It was time to wrap things up in the workshop and go in to help Emma with the final touches for the festivities that evening.

The helpers had different jobs they did for Nicholas and Emma. The workshop was everyone's favorite place because it was such fun to see all the toys Nicholas would make. They often would talk among themselves, why did he do it? Make all the toys every year when they had no children? No one could come up with the answer. They were just glad they were inside on this coldest of nights.

But a few of the helpers had to be outside watching the animals. The small barn had 2 cows, 2 pigs, 6 chickens and 8 reindeer. They all needed hay and feed for the night before the helpers could call it a day. The sheep were out on the hillside being tended by 3 of the helpers. They were huddled around a fire, keeping as warm as they could. Soon they would herd the sheep back to the barn so they could go to the party too. But all of a sudden there was a light.

The light was so bright they had to cover their eyes. They were very afraid. But then they realized the light was not just a star, it was a star like they had not seen before. It not only was bright but it was actually shaped like part of it was pointing to something or someplace on earth. It was an interesting shape, something they had not seen before. They decided to herd the sheep back to the barn and get cleaned up for Emma's famous anniversary meal. Maybe Nicholas would know what kind of star it was. He knew all about the stars in the sky.

Nicholas had just finished bathing and getting dressed for the party. He was helping Emma set the big table in the dining room. She always used her best dishes and silverware for the yearly party. They were discussing the storm and if it would affect the hens laying eggs. Suddenly there was a flash of light so bright, they both covered their eyes. They both ran to the window and off in the distance, on the hillside where the shepherds were tending the sheep, they could see a very bright light.

The meal was delicious, cooked to perfection, but they were all so excited about the strange looking star on the hillside, they barely noticed it. Even though they didn't understand the significance of what had happened, they all knew it was something important. After everyone had left and Emma had finished the dishes, Nicholas and Emma sat in the living room before the fire and talked about the star. They talked late into the night and almost forgot about their gift exchange. But Nicholas was excited for Emma to see his carved mother, father and baby. She loved the carving and wondered what or who they were. He loved his scarf and knew it had taken Emma many hours to crochet it, but it was the carved figurines that Nicholas had made for Emma, that intrigued them both. Nicholas told her he had no idea why he had carved a baby lying in a straw bed with both parents kneeling. Was there a connection to the star they had all seen? They knew all the questions they had wouldn't be answered that night. They decided to get a good night's sleep and try to figure it all out in the morning.

She could see the star from her window as she slowly opened her eyes in the pre-dawn hours. It was the unique shape that got Emma out of bed, put on her robe and went to the kitchen to make coffee. The star seemed to be everywhere, for she could see it from every room and every direction.

Nicholas could smell the coffee and knew cinnamon rolls were waiting for him. He meandered out to the kitchen and noticed too, the star. He knew all the stars and where they all belonged in the majestic sky, but never had he seen this one. As expected, Emma was sitting at the table, coffee and rolls waiting. She looked perplexed and he knew she was wondering about the star, too. While eating, she told him how the star seemed to draw her to it. He agreed he had the same feeling. They both knew what they had to do. But they just couldn't say it out loud. Not yet. Soon enough the time would come. For now, they had lots to do to get ready.

The day passed quickly. Nicholas felt compelled to take all the toys he had made with him. The helpers very carefully, helped him pack each toy to assure it wouldn't break. Emma, in the meantime, cooked and baked enough food to last at least 2 weeks. Hopefully, it would be enough. All their clothes were washed, neatly folded and ready to go. The sleigh was being cleaned by the helpers for the long trip. Even though, it wasn't all that big, the more items Emma and Nicholas packed, there seem to be more space available. No one understood or could explain how the sleigh seemed to have a never-ending bottom. The reindeer would need food, too, and a special compartment in the back held enough hay for a couple of weeks. The packing was done. They were ready to "Follow The Star".

They traveled all day, only stopping long enough for a bite to eat and to feed the reindeer. Not knowing where they would sleep that night, they started looking for a place. About that time, they both saw a farmstead and headed for it, hoping the family there would have room for them to stay overnight. When they knocked on the door, a little boy answered it. His mother was right behind him and invited them in. Emma brought in some of the food she made and they soon had supper and a place to sleep. The next morning they were up early, but before they left, Nicholas left the little boy one of his homemade toys.

The next several days and nights were very similar, finding a family to stay with, bringing the family food for a bed to sleep in and leaving toys for the children before they left the next morning. As they traveled they noticed less snow than where they were from. They also noticed how different the animals were. They were big and had funny humps in their back where the people rode. Their sleigh looked funny on the dry sand. They certainly got funny looks from everyone.

They knew they were close to their destination. The star was almost totally over them. Not far up the road they saw a small town. They asked a passerby what the name of the town was. They noticed that all the men in this part of the world wore strange clothes. They didn't wear pants, but a robe similar to a long dress or gown that a woman would wear. And they covered their heads too. Not with a hat but a cloth that came down past their shoulders. He told them the name of the town was Bethlehem. What a strange name, but it seemed like the star was directly over the small town so that's where they headed.

When they arrived in Bethlehem, they went to an inn to see if there was a room. They were told there was no room, but several people were staying in the barn. They decided to see if there was room for them and needed to feed the reindeer. When they entered the barn, they knew they had found what they were looking for. There was the mother, father and baby in a manger, just like the carving Nicholas had made. They both saw others there kneeling before the baby. Some men from a place called "the East" brought gifts. Quickly, Emma and Nicholas brought in food from the sleigh for all to enjoy. They also brought in gifts Nicholas had made, and gave them to the baby. They found out the names of the parents, Mary and Joseph. The baby was a King, called Jesus. He had come into this world as a baby and would later die on a cross to save the world from their sins.

After spending a few days with the Holy Family, Nicholas and Emma knew they needed to get back home. They knelt for the last time in front of Jesus and knew this tiny baby would change the world forever. They felt very blessed they were a part of it. On their way back north, they continued to stay with families, giving food and toys everywhere they went. When they finally got back home, they decided they would travel again the next year on Dec 25 bringing toys to families along the way. The baby Jesus was born on Dec 25 and the gifts would be given to children around the world to remember the gift the Savior brought to the world, eternal life!

CPSIA information can be obtained at www.ICGtesting.com
Printed in the USA
LVOW05s0442220915

455127LV00019B/545/P